HOW TO BE A BBC

SUPERTATO

SIMON & SCHUSTER
London New York Sydney Toronto New Delhi

SIMON & SCHUSTER
Celebrating 100 Years of Publishing Since 1924
First published in Great Britain in 2024 by Simon & Schuster UK Ltd
1st Floor, 222 Gray's Inn Road, London WC1X 8HB

A CIP catalogue record for this book is available from the British Library upon request

ISBN: 978-1-3985-3031-7 (PB)
ISBN: 978-1-3985-3032-4 (EB)

Printed in China
1 3 5 7 9 10 8 6 4 2

ATTENTION, SUPER-READERS!

Today, Supertato is wowing the Grape Kids with a tour of Tato Tower. The Grape Kids are **EXCITED**.

"What does this red button do?" asks a Grape Kid.

"Good question! That button opens the door to where I keep my super capes," Supertato replies, swishing his super cape. The Grape Kids are **VERY** impressed.

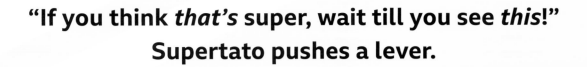

"If you think *that's* super, wait till you see *this*!"
Supertato pushes a lever.

The Grape Kids clap their hands as Supertato
shows them how he launches himself from Tato Tower.
"Now gather round," Supertato tells them. "It's time for my super video!"

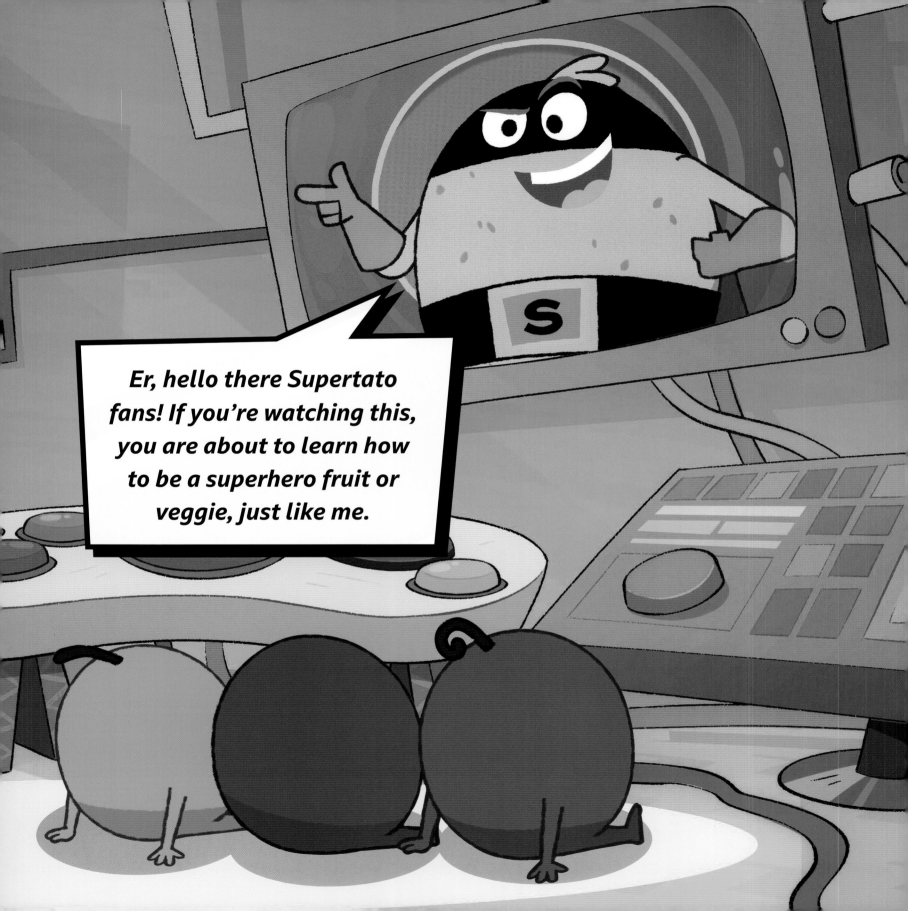

Being a superhero would be exhausting if it wasn't for super fitness!

A super veggie always has to stay super fit. That's why it's important to do lots of super exercise.

Sometimes being super fit isn't enough. A superhero must have super gadgets too! Like the Tato Belt!

But wait . . . aren't we forgetting something that no superhero is complete without? Can you guess?

Meanwhile, on screen, Supertato explains he needs super sidekicks and his veggie friends.

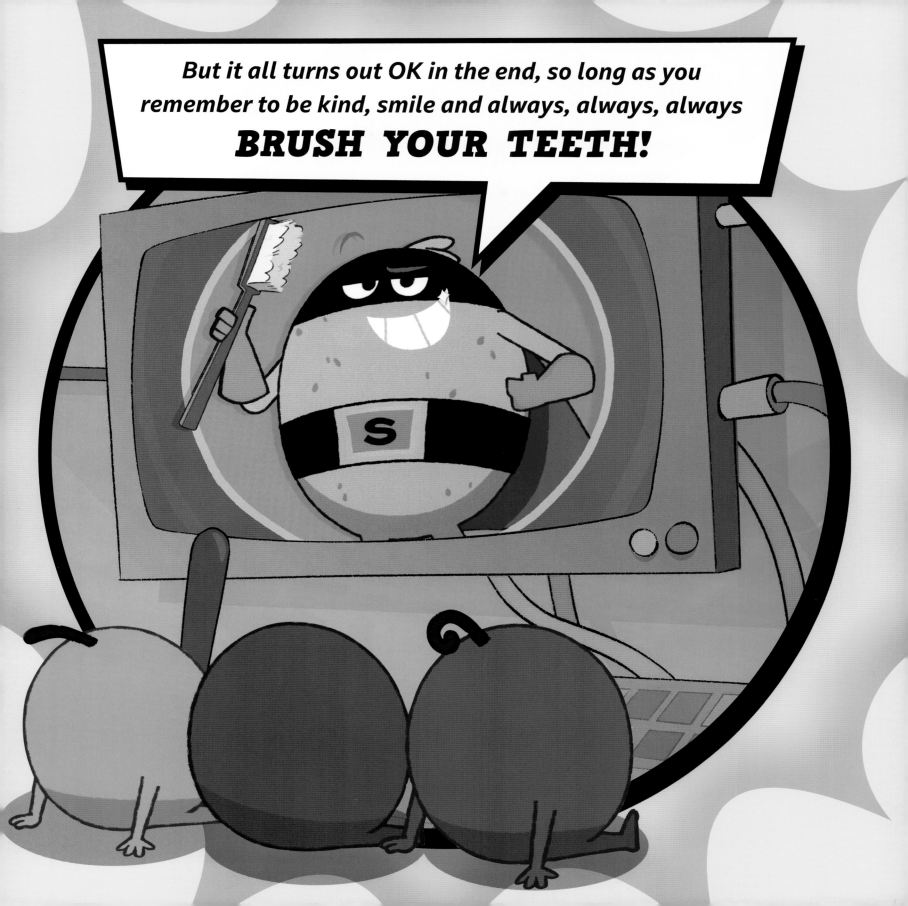

"And that is the end of my super video.
Does anyone have any questions?" asks Supertato.

"I have a question!" Evil Pea shouts.

"Get back, everyone!" shouts Supertato.
"What is brown and flies through the air screaming?"
cackles Evil Pea.

"Oooh, I don't know. What IS brown and flies
through the air screaming?" asks Supertato.

ARGHHHHHHHHHHHHHH!

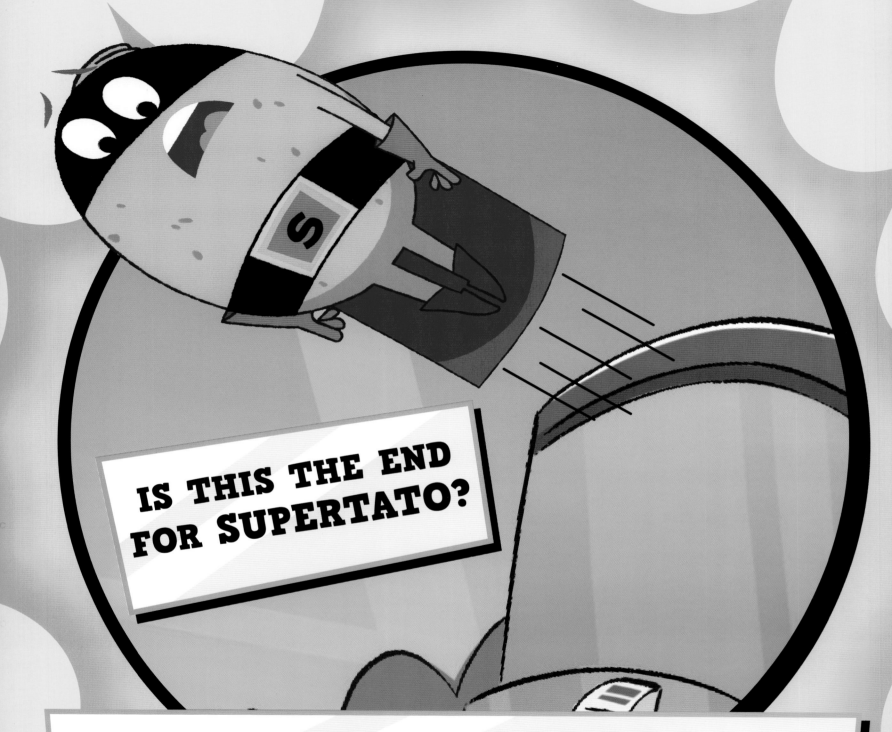

IS THIS THE END FOR SUPERTATO?

"PWAH ha ha ha ha!" Evil Pea laughs.
"Noooooooooooo!" shout the Grape Kids.
"Finally," cackles Evil Pea, "the Tato Tower is mine, ALL MINE!"

But the Grape Kids aren't finished . . .

**"Not so fast, Pea! Hold it right there!" yells a Grape Kid.
Evil Pea grits her teeth. "My name is EVIL Pea!"**

. . . knocks her to the floor.
Suddenly Evil Pea spots a Grape Kid standing by the lever.
"Don't you dare! No . . . no, no, no, no, no!"

"Oooh, I dare, I dare! **GRAPE KID BOUNCE!**"
The Grape Kid jumps up and down in excitement and . . .

HHHHHH!

Unaware of the Grape Kids' victory, Supertato rushes back to Tato Tower, ready to save the day. "Supertato to the . . ."

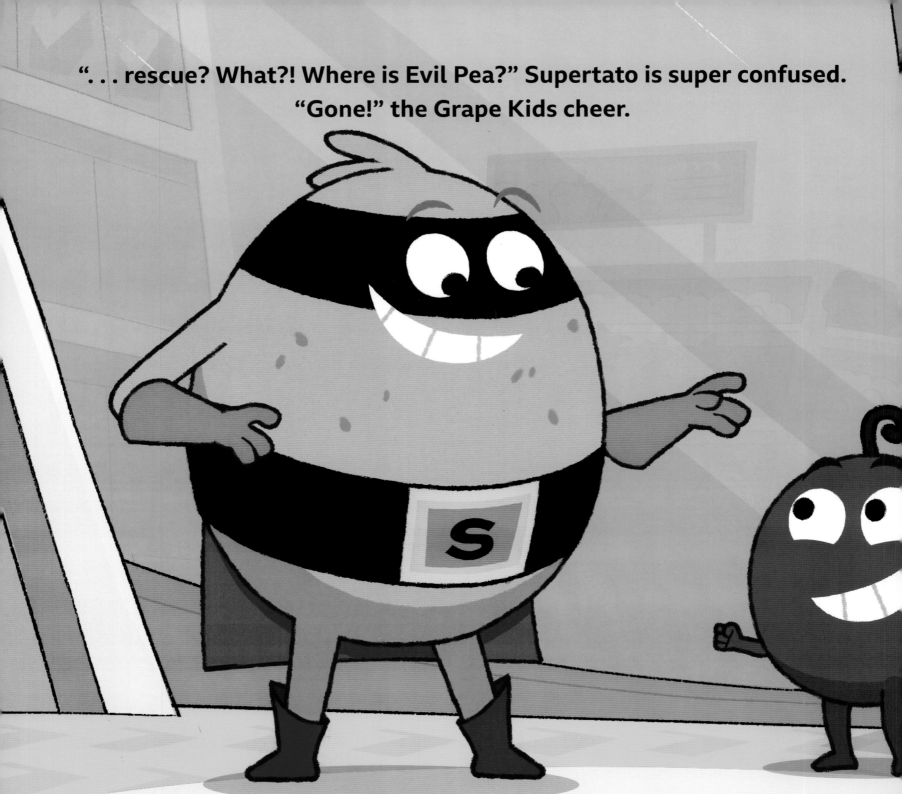

". . . rescue? What?! Where is Evil Pea?" Supertato is super confused.
"Gone!" the Grape Kids cheer.

"Looks like your super training video paid off," they tell Supertato.
"Well done everyone," Supertato smiles. "That is really . . ."